Teachers, librarians, and kids from
across Canada are talking about the
Canadian Flyer Adventures.
Here's what some of them had to say:

Great Canadian historical content, excellent illustrations,
and superb closing historical facts (I love the kids'
commentary!). ~ *SARA S., TEACHER, ONTARIO*

As a teacher–librarian I welcome this series with open
arms. It fills the gap for Canadian historical adventures
at an early reading level! There's fast action, interesting,
believable characters, and great historical information.
~ *MARGARET L., TEACHER–LIBRARIAN, BRITISH COLUMBIA*

The *Canadian Flyer Adventures* will transport young
readers to different eras of our past with their appealing
topics. Thank goodness there are more artifacts in that old
dresser ... they are sure to lead to even more escapades.
~ *SALLY B., TEACHER–LIBRARIAN, MANITOBA*

When I shared the book with a grade 1–2 teacher at
my school, she enjoyed the book, noting that her students
would find it appealing because of the action-adventure
and short chapters. ~ *HEATHER J., TEACHER AND
LIBRARIAN, NOVA SCOTIA*

Newly independent readers will fly through
each *Canadian Flyer Adventure*, and be asking for
the next installment! Children will enjoy the fast-paced
narrative, the personalities of the main characters, and
the drama of the dangerous situations the children
find themselves in. ~ *PAM L., LIBRARIAN, ONTARIO*

I love the fact that these are Canadian adventures—kids should know how exciting Canadian history is. Emily and Matt are regular kids, full of curiosity, and I can see readers relating to them. ~ *JEAN K., TEACHER, ONTARIO*

What kids told us:

I would like to have the chance to ride on a magical sled and have adventures. ~ *EMMANUEL*

I would like to tell the author that her book is amazing, incredible, awesome, and a million times better than any book I've read. ~ *MARIA*

I would recommend the *Canadian Flyer Adventures* series to other kids so they could learn about Canada too. The book is just the right length and hard to put down. ~ *PAUL*

The books I usually read are the full-of-fact encyclopedias. This book is full of interesting ideas that simply grab me. ~ *ELEANOR*

At the end of the book Matt and Emily say they are going on another adventure. I'm very interested in where they are going next! ~ *ALEX*

I like when Emily and Matt fly into the sky on a sled towards a new adventure. I can't wait for the next book! ~ *JI SANG*

SOS!
Titanic!

Frieda Wishinsky

Illustrated by Jean-Paul Eid

MAPLE
TREE
PRESS

For my friend, Helen Elliot

Many thanks to the hard-working Owlkids team, for their insightful comments and steadfast support. Special thanks to Jean-Paul Eid and Barb Kelly for their engaging and energetic illustrations and design.

Maple Tree Press books are published by Owlkids Books Inc.
10 Lower Spadina Avenue, Suite 400, Toronto, Ontario M5V 2Z2
www.owlkids.com

Text © 2010 Frieda Wishinsky   Illustrations © 2010 Jean-Paul Eid

Distributed in Canada by Raincoast Books
9050 Shaughnessy Street, Vancouver, British Columbia V6P 6E5

Distributed in the United States by Publishers Group West
1700 Fourth Street, Berkeley, California 94710

Library and Archives Canada Cataloguing in Publication

Wishinsky, Frieda
SOS! Titanic! / Frieda Wishinsky ; illustrated by Jean-Paul Eid.

(Canadian flyer adventures ; 14)
ISBN 978-1-897349-77-9 (bound).--ISBN 978-1-897349-78-6 (pbk.)

1. Titanic (Steamship)--Juvenile fiction. I. Eid, Jean-Paul
II. Title. III. Series: Wishinsky, Frieda. Canadian flyer adventures ; 14.

PS8595.I834S68 2010   jC813'.54   C2009-905310-1

Library of Congress Control Number: 2009935528

 Canada Council   Conseil des Arts
for the Arts   du Canada

 ONTARIO ARTS COUNCIL
CONSEIL DES ARTS DE L'ONTARIO

We acknowledge the financial support of the Canada Council for the Arts, the Ontario Arts Council, the Government of Canada through the Canada Book Fund (CBF), and the Government of Ontario through the Ontario Media Development Corporation's Book Initiative for our publishing activities.

Printed in Canada
Ancient Forest Friendly: Printed on 100% Post-Consumer Recycled Paper

Manufactured by Friesens Corporation
Manufactured in Altona, MB, Canada in March, 2010
Job# 53662

A   B   C   D   E   F

CONTENTS

HOW IT ALL BEGAN

Emily and Matt couldn't believe their luck. They discovered an old dresser full of strange objects in the tower of Emily's house. They also found a note from Emily's Great-Aunt Miranda: "The sled is yours. Fly it to wonderful adventures."

They found a sled right behind the dresser! When they sat on it, shimmery gold words appeared:

> *Rub the leaf*
> *Three times fast.*
> *Soon you'll fly*
> *To the past.*

The sled rose over Emily's house. It flew over their town of Glenwood. It sailed out of a cloud and into the past. Their adventures on the flying sled had begun! Where will the sled take them next? Turn the page to find out.

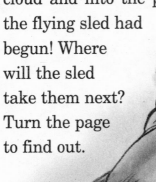

1

Titanic Crazy

The phone rang. Emily raced to answer it.

"Hi, Em." It was her best friend Matt. "I finally finished. Come and see it!"

"Come and see what?"

"You'll see. It's awesome."

"Awesome? I'll be right over."

Emily ran to Matt's house.

He was waiting at the front door. "This way!" he said.

Emily followed Matt to his room. A large cardboard box was sitting on his desk.

He lifted the box. "What do you think?"

"Wow!" exclaimed Emily. "That's a big ship."

"It's not just any big ship. Don't you recognize it?"

"No."

"Come on, Em. It was the most awesome ship ever built. Well, that is till it sank."

Emily's eyes widened. "Is that a model of the *Titanic*?"

"You bet. Check out the name on the side."

Emily looked at the side of the ship. There it was in gold letters: TITANIC.

"It was the jewel of the White Star Line," said Matt. "It was built in Belfast, Ireland, and finished in 1912. It sailed from England on April 10th and left Ireland on April 11th for New York. You want to know more?"

"Sure." Emily grinned. "You sound like you know everything about the *Titanic*.

But tell me some more, not everything."

"I don't know everything. All I know is that I love the *Titanic*. I'm..."

"*Titanic* crazy?" said Emily, laughing.

"Yep."

"I read a book about the *Titanic*. I knew the ship was going to sink, but I still bit my nails for the last three chapters," said Emily.

"Wouldn't it be amazing to fly to the *Titanic*?" said Matt. "Maybe we could stop the ship from sinking."

"Yeah, right. We can't change history. No one can."

"We don't know that for sure. What if we tell the captain that he has to watch out for icebergs? We'd tell him that if he doesn't, his ship is doomed. We can even tell him the exact time the *Titanic* will hit the iceberg off the coast of Newfoundland, and lots of other facts."

"But what if he doesn't believe us? I don't want to see all those poor people go down with the ship. That would be awful."

Matt looked at his model. He rubbed his hand across the word *Titanic*. "If we can find something about the *Titanic* in your Great-Aunt Miranda's dresser, then the sled will take us there. Even if we can't stop the ship from sinking, we might save someone. It's worth a try. And I thought I saw something *Titanic* in the third drawer. Come on, Em! It would be fantastic to be on the *Titanic*, even for a little while."

"I don't remember seeing anything in the dresser from the ship, but you're right. Walking around the *Titanic* would be amazing."

"Maybe we could even go swimming," said Matt.

Emily shivered. "Are you kidding? The

Atlantic Ocean is freezing in April. There were icebergs everywhere!"

"We wouldn't swim in the Atlantic. There was a pool on the *Titanic*. If you were in First Class, you could go swimming for twenty-five cents."

"That would be fun, but what I'd really like is to walk down the Grand Staircase." Emily stood up. She lifted an imaginary long skirt and walked across the room as if she were an actress on the red carpet. "I'll draw a picture in my sketchbook of me walking like this and waving to my fans."

Matt laughed. "And I'll record everything on my recorder."

"Even the sound of the *Titanic* hitting the iceberg?"

"If we can't stop it, I'd at least be recording history."

2

April 14, 1912

Emily and Matt dashed up the rickety stairs to the tower room.

Emily ran over to the mahogany dresser. She opened the third drawer and peered in. "Nothing *Titanic* here."

"Try another drawer," said Matt.

Emily opened the second drawer. "Nope. Not here either."

"Try the first drawer."

"Okay. Wow! Look at this!" Emily pulled out a thick piece of paper and showed Matt.

R.M.S. "TITANIC"

"It's a first-class menu from the *Titanic*. Look! You could eat ten courses for dinner. Maybe the *Titanic* sank because people ate too much!"

Matt laughed. "Yeah, right. They didn't have to eat everything on the menu, but in the early 1900s rich people loved gigantic meals."

"Well, this is a gigantic meal."

Matt examined the menu. "They had three courses of meat in First Class! One piece of roast chicken is all I can eat for supper."

"I bet by the fifth course you're so stuffed, you have to run three times around the ship for exercise. Then you can come back and eat more. After all, you can't miss the tenth course—dessert!" Emily closed her eyes. "Mmm. I want one of those chocolate painted eclairs right now."

7

"So what are we waiting for? Let's fly!" said Matt.

"But remember, we can't eat too much or the sled might not be able to lift us up and fly us back home," said Emily, laughing.

"Don't worry. I could never eat that much." Matt pulled the sled out from behind the dresser. The friends hopped on, and Emily rubbed the maple leaf in front of the sled.

Soon the magic words appeared.

Rub the leaf
Three times fast.
Soon you'll fly
To the past.

As soon as they did, the sled was engulfed in fog. When it lifted, they flew over Emily's house, over Glenwood, and toward a fluffy white cloud.

"Every time we fly," said Matt, "my heart pounds like crazy."

"My heart pounds, too," said Emily. "We're so high up. And we never know what will happen."

"Sometimes when I look down, my stomach feels like it will flip out of my body!"

"Hold on to your stomach, Matt! Here comes the cloud."

The sled flew into the fluffy white cloud.

When it burst out, it was late afternoon and they were flying over the Atlantic. Below them sailed the *Titanic*.

"Wow! It's even more beautiful in real life than in the movies," said Emily.

Matt sighed. "Poor *Titanic*."

"Maybe not," said Emily. "Emily and Matt to the rescue!"

3

3:00 P.M.

The sled landed beside the rail on a lower deck of the ship.

"Hey! This isn't First Class," said Emily, looking around.

"I bet it's Third Class," said Matt. "You can get to Second and First Class from the bridge deck, which is above us."

"Let's go up."

"Why don't we check out Third Class first? Then we can see more of the ship."

"We'd better keep track of the time and

keep the sled with us," said Emily. "We need it safe and handy in case—"

"I know," said Matt, peering over the railing. "It's freezing in the Atlantic. No one would last long down there, even an Olympic swimmer."

Emily shivered. "I don't even want to think about that. Come on. Let's look around."

As the friends turned away from the railing, a boy of about eight wearing a short grey jacket, long pants, and a cap rushed past them. He crouched behind a wooden bench.

"Shh," he whispered. "Don't tell."

"Don't tell what?" Emily whispered back.

"That I'm here. We're playing hide-and-seek. I don't want to get caught and be It."

"Ready or not, here I come," a girl called out. Then she said, "Got you! You're It."

"Phew! She caught someone else," said the boy under the bench. He popped up. "Are you lost? You don't look like you belong in Third Class in those fancy clothes."

Emily and Matt glanced down. Emily wore a long purple dress with a round collar, high button shoes, and a purple ribbon around her ponytail.

Matt wore a blue suit, a white shirt, pants that ended below his knees, and button-up shoes.

"Yes. We're from up there," said Matt. "We just wanted to see every part of the *Titanic*."

"Isn't it a wonderful ship?" said the boy. "My mum and dad saved for two years so we could sail on it. We're going to live in America. We'll help my uncle on his farm in Pennsylvania. My name's Lou."

"I'm Emily."

"I'm Matt."

"Glad to meet you. Do you want to play?" asked Lou.

"That would be great, except...what time is it?" asked Emily.

Lou shook his head. "I don't know."

"We'd better go," said Matt.

"Come back down and we'll play some other time," said Lou.

"That would be fun," said Matt, "except that..."

Lou frowned. "Your parents don't want you to play with third-class kids, right?"

"No. We can play with anyone we want. It's just that—" said Matt.

"What?" asked Lou.

Emily took a deep breath. "If something happens to the *Titanic*—if it hits an iceberg, promise you'll run to a lifeboat. Don't wait for anything. Okay?"

Lou slapped his thigh and howled with laughter. "Nothing is going to happen to the *Titanic*. It's unsinkable."

"Promise us anyway," said Matt.

Lou rolled his eyes. "You two are strange."

Emily smiled. "Maybe we are, but please remember what we said."

"I'll remember because it's the silliest thing I've ever heard."

4

4:00 P.M.

Matt picked up the sled to carry it. There was a gate in front of the stairs. It looked like it was there to stop third-class passengers from going up to the second-class and first-class promenade deck. But someone had left it open.

Matt and Emily waved to Lou and scurried up the stairs. When they reached the second-class promenade deck, Matt bent over to put the sled down and collided with a woman.

"Oh, dear. I'm so sorry," she said. "Are you okay?"

"I think so," said Matt rubbing his head. "But my head's a little sore."

"My head is sore, too," said the woman. She was in her mid-twenties and wore a long blue dress with a blue shawl. "I've been frantic looking for my scarf and I didn't see you. My fiancé gave it to me. It's silver and blue silk. Have you seen it?"

"Is this it?" asked Emily. She leaned under a deck chair and pulled out a scarf tangled in the chair's leg.

"Oh yes! Yes!" The woman's eyes sparkled. "Thank you. Now I can face my Harry again. We are to be married in Canada soon. I even have my wedding dress with me on the ship."

"Wow! We're from Canada, too," said Emily.

"I was born in Nova Scotia, but Harry lives in British Columbia. We'll be married there. My name is Hilda Slayter."

17

"I'm Emily and this is Matt. What does your dress look like?"

Hilda's eyes twinkled. "Would you like to see it?" she asked.

"Yes," said Emily.

"I assume you're not as interested in wedding dresses as Emily," said Hilda, smiling at Matt.

"I don't mind seeing it. And Emily and I always stick together."

The two friends followed Hilda to her room on the saloon deck. "I'm sharing these quarters with my friend Florence," she explained as she opened her stateroom door.

The room had two beds. Each bed had a carved wooden headboard. In between the two beds stood a dresser with a large carved oval mirror. There was also a small couch in the room.

Emily and Matt sat on the couch while Hilda yanked a large trunk out from under her bed. She opened the trunk. She lifted up layers of tissue paper and pulled out a long satin dress laced with pearls.

"It's beautiful!" said Emily.

Hilda beamed. "I plan to keep it forever and pass it on to my daughter. I hope she will pass it on to her daughter."

"That's a great idea," said Emily. "But... just in case something happens to the *Titanic*, don't go back and get your dress. Just run to a lifeboat. Okay?"

Hilda's eyes widened. She stared at Emily, "Why would you say such a strange thing? Nothing will happen to the *Titanic*. And if it did, I would take my dress with me to the lifeboat. I could never leave it behind."

Hilda looked at her watch. "Oh dear. It's almost five. I really must go. I promised Florence I'd stroll with her on the deck before dinner."

They hurried out of the stateroom. Hilda waved goodbye and walked off to join her friend.

"She thinks I'm nuts," said Emily.

"Maybe," said Matt, "but maybe she'll remember what you said. I just wish we could make people believe us about the *Titanic*."

"I know what we can do!" said Emily. "Why don't you show your recorder to the next person we meet? That will prove we're from the future."

A girl tapped Emily on the shoulder. "Did you just say you're from the future?" she asked.

Emily and Matt turned. The girl was about ten. She had curly red hair and freckles. She wore a long navy blue dress with a white collar and a navy blue ribbon in her hair. She pointed at them and laughed. "That's the funniest thing I've heard all day! I bet the next thing you'll say is that you can fly."

5

5:00 P.M.

"We are from the future and we'll prove it," said Matt. He pulled his recorder out of his pants pocket. "This is a digital recorder. You can hear people's voices on it."

The girl waved her hand as if dismissing Matt's words. "That's just a little metal box. And if you're from the future, then I'm from the moon. And I'm not."

Matt turned the recorder on. "This is Matt speaking," he said. Then he played his voice back.

The girl's eyes widened. "That's a good trick," she said. "It's almost as good as when I saw a man pull a rabbit out of his hat."

"Here, you talk into the recorder and I'll play your voice back," said Matt.

Matt pressed the on button and the girl spoke into the recorder. "My name is Sally and I'm on the *Titanic* with two silly children!"

Matt flipped the recorder off and on again. Sally gasped as she listened to her voice. "That's fantastic, but it still doesn't prove anything."

Matt sighed.

"Look," said Sally. "It's a terrific trick. You two are fun. Do you want to explore?"

"Sure," said Emily. "I'm Emily. Matt and I want to go up to First Class."

"Me, too! Let's go!" said Sally.

The children climbed the stairs to the first-class promenade deck. When they reached the top, Emily shivered. "It's getting colder out. I wanted to go swimming but I'm too cold now. Anyway, I don't have a bathing suit."

"Let's go to the gymnasium," suggested Sally. "I hear they have a mechanical horse and camel you can ride on."

"Awesome," said Matt. "But where's the gymnasium?"

"Let's ask that boy over there," said Emily.

A boy of about nine in short grey pants and high boots was walking briskly down the deck.

"Excuse me," said Emily. "How do we get to the gymnasium?"

The boy stared at them. "Who are you? I've never seen any of you and I know all the children in First Class. You don't belong here."

"We just want to see the gymnasium," said Sally.

The boy glared at them. "The gymnasium is only open till 3:30, so you can't see it. If you don't leave right now, I'm going to call the steward and he'll make you leave." The boy opened his mouth to yell.

"You'll do no such thing, Arthur," said a plump woman with a booming voice. Her huge hat was covered in feathers, and her long grey coat had a fluffy fur collar. "That is no way to speak to anyone. Your mother would be horrified at your bad manners."

Arthur wrinkled his nose at the woman.

"My mother would not be horrified, Mrs. Brown. She thinks people should stay where they belong."

"Well, these children belong here now. They are my guests. So off you go, Arthur. Come, children. Follow me."

6

6:00 P.M.

"Arthur is only nine and he's already convinced he owns the world. I can't imagine what he'll be like when he grows up," said Mrs. Brown.

"Thanks for letting us stay here," said Emily.

"It's my pleasure, dear. You children are not harming anyone. You were just curious about First Class."

"I'm Emily. This is Matt and Sally, and we're more than curious," said Emily. "We have to talk to the captain tonight."

"It's very important," said Matt.

"Well, it just so happens that Captain Smith may dine at my table tonight. Why don't you three join me for dinner, if it's all right with your family?"

"They won't mind. Thank you! That's awesome!" said Matt.

Sally sighed. "I would love to have dinner in First Class, too, but I promised my aunt I'd have dinner with her. I'd better get back now. She'll wonder where I am. Thanks for being so kind, Mrs. Brown."

"Goodbye, Sally. Now, I really must sit down on that deck chair while you children say your goodbyes. My feet are killing me in these new shoes. I don't know why I bought them." Mrs. Brown hobbled over to a chair.

Sally turned to Matt and Emily. "Come visit with me tomorrow again."

Emily and Matt looked at each other. How could they tell Sally that the *Titanic* would not be sailing tomorrow? She still didn't believe that they were from the future. Why would she believe that the ship was going to collide with an iceberg and sink in a few hours? But she was their friend now. They had to warn her.

"We'd love to play with you again tomorrow, but something will happen tonight that will change everything," said Matt.

"So you're not only from the future," said Sally, laughing. "You're also fortune tellers."

"I know it's hard to believe, but in a few hours the *Titanic* is going to hit an iceberg and sink. We don't want anything to happen to you. Please, please get to a lifeboat when it happens," said Emily.

"If the ship hits an iceberg, I will," said Sally. "If a whale smashes into the ship and pokes a hole through it, I'll get into a lifeboat, too. And if a shark leaps out of the water and tries to eat me, I'll run so fast that he won't be able to take even a little bite."

"I know you think we're making this all up, Sally, but please remember what we told you," Matt said.

"You two are the funniest and oddest children I've ever met. Don't forget. Come to Second Class and we'll play again tomorrow."

Sally turned and sped down the staircase to Second Class.

"What now?" said Matt.

"We have to tell the captain about the iceberg. He's the only person who can stop this ship. Isn't it lucky we're going to have dinner with him? Maybe our luck is changing. Maybe the *Titanic*'s luck is changing, too!"

7

6:30 P.M.

Matt and Emily ran over to the deck chair where Mrs. Brown was seated. She was speaking to an elderly couple.

"Ah, here you are," said Mrs. Brown. "Ida and Isidor, let me introduce you to my two young friends, Emily and Matt. I'm sure they've heard of your store—Macy's."

Emily's jaw dropped. "I love Macy's. I went to visit my cousins in New York, and we went shopping there. It's gigantic. I almost got lost in the underwear department!"

Everyone howled with laughter. "I'm delighted you like our store," said Mrs. Straus. "And I'm glad you found your way out of underwear."

"And I love your parade. I always watch part of it on the news on Thanksgiving," said Matt.

"We don't have a parade," said Mrs. Straus.

"You must be confusing it with another event," said Mr. Straus. He turned to his wife. "But this is an interesting idea, Ida. I must bring it up to my staff when we return home."

Matt glanced at Emily. He knew what she was thinking. The Macy's parades probably didn't start until after 1912. That's why Mr. and Mrs. Straus didn't know about them. And if the *Titanic* sank, Mr. and Mrs. Straus might never make it back to their store and be part of any parade—or anything.

"Now, children. It's time we head toward the first-class dining saloon and dinner," said Mrs. Brown. She stood up.

"Saloon? Isn't that a bar where people drink liquor?" asked Emily.

"Yes," said Mrs. Brown. "It's also what our first-class dining room is called. I'll tell the head waiter to set two extra settings at my table. They allow children in the dining saloon, but not a sled, I'm afraid." She winked at Emily and Matt.

"Can we leave our sled in your stateroom?" asked Emily.

"Certainly. We'll take the lift to my stateroom. I'll change into comfortable shoes and then we'll go down for dinner. Ida and Isidor, we'll see you at dinner."

With a wave to Mr. and Mrs. Straus, Emily and Matt followed Mrs. Brown down the deck.

She opened a door and Emily and Matt gasped. There, right in front of them, was the magnificent Grand Staircase. It was made of oak and wrought iron, and there was a glass dome overhead to let the natural light stream in. A clock was set into the carved wall at the top of the staircase, and a fat cherub stood on a pedestal at the bottom.

"I've been dreaming of walking down this staircase," said Emily.

"Well, go ahead. Do it!" said Mrs. Brown.

Emily raced up to the top of the first landing. She picked up one end of her purple skirt and slowly walked down the stairs. She smiled and waved, and Mrs. Brown and Matt applauded.

Then Matt began to sing, "Here she comes. Emily Bing! The famous actress from Glenwood!"

"Glenwood? What kind of place is Glenwood?" said an elegantly dressed woman in a long blue silk gown walking behind Emily. The woman was holding the arm of a man in a black suit.

Emily stopped walking and blushed. "Glenwood is a town in Ontario."

The woman sniffed. "Oh. Canada." She gave Emily a disapproving look and headed toward a metal door near the staircase. "That awful Mrs. Brown must have put the child up to it. Such ridiculous behaviour," the woman said to her companion.

Before Mrs. Brown or the kids could reply, the metal doors opened and the couple hurried inside. Then the doors clanged shut.

"Wow! That's the lift!" said Matt. "It's a fancy elevator!"

"And those are rude people," said Mrs. Brown.

"They had no right saying those mean things to you, Mrs. Brown," said Emily.

"Not everyone on the ship approves of me. Some people think I'm brash and loud. But lovely people like Ida and Isidor Straus are not swayed by where you come from. They respect who you are as a person."

"My parents say the same thing," said Emily. "They believe it's who you are inside that counts, not how much money you have."

"There are mean-spirited people with buckets of money on this ship and lovely, thoughtful people who happen to be poor. The *Titanic* has all kinds of people," said Mrs. Brown. "Ah, here's our lift. It will take us to my stateroom. I can't wait to take these shoes off. Why did I let that saleslady in London convince me to buy such uncomfortable shoes? Who cares if they're the height of fashion?"

8

7:00 P.M.

Emily and Matt placed the sled in a corner of Mrs. Brown's large stateroom. As Mrs. Brown slipped off her shoes, Emily quickly sketched herself parading down the Grand Staircase.

"I like your drawing," said Mrs. Brown. "Now let's eat a delicious *Titanic* dinner!"

The lift dropped them off in front of the dining saloon.

"Wow!" said Emily when they stepped out. "Look at the glass dome in here!"

"And check out those fancy windows and these big green chairs," said Matt. "Two people could fit into each of the chairs."

"Two people your size, Matt," said Mrs. Brown, chuckling. "One chair is just right for me."

Mrs. Brown headed for a table. Emily and Matt followed. They passed a table where some men were looking at a menu. Emily nudged Matt in the arm and whispered, "There's our menu!"

They had just sat down beside Mrs. Brown when a waiter approached. "Pardon me, Madam," he said to Mrs. Brown. "I have a note from the captain."

Mrs. Brown scanned the note. "I'm afraid the captain didn't realize till this afternoon that a dinner party is being given in his honour in the A La Carte restaurant tonight.

He promises to join us tomorrow for dinner. Come back again tomorrow, children, and you can talk to him about your important matter."

"Tomorrow!" cried Emily. "Tomorrow will be too late."

"I know it's disappointing not to speak to the captain tonight. He's charming and this is his last voyage."

Matt gulped. "We know."

"Yes. The word is out. He's retiring after this trip, and I know he'll miss the sea. I like the sea, too, as long as I don't have to swim in

it," said Mrs. Brown, chuckling.

Matt glanced at Emily. They had to warn Mrs. Brown about the iceberg. Swimming in the sea might be a real possibility soon.

"Mrs. Brown," said Emily. "If the ship hits an iceberg tonight, don't wait. Head for the lifeboats, okay?"

Mrs. Brown patted Emily on the shoulder. "If something like that was to happen, my dear, I'd jump into a lifeboat quicker than a frog into a pond. I have no intention of swimming to New York. I'd even row the lifeboat myself.

You children have probably been reading books about disasters at sea. Don't worry. Nothing like that will happen here. Eat your dinner. The food on this ship is out of this world!"

Despite the delicious food, Emily and Matt could barely eat. They couldn't stop thinking that in a few hours the *Titanic* was going to sink. And no matter how hard they tried, no one believed them. Not Lou, or Hilda Slayter, or Sally, or Mrs. Brown. No one.

And now they couldn't even speak to Captain Smith, the one person who really mattered. They couldn't leave dinner to look for him either. It would be rude to Mrs. Brown. But they had to find the captain, and *soon*.

"Come on you two. Eat!" Mrs. Brown coaxed them. "Each course here is tastier than the last. And dessert is the next course."

Emily's eyes lit up "I'll have some dessert. I could never miss that."

The waiter brought the desserts out. The eclairs looked as scrumptious as Emily and Matt imagined. They tasted as scrumptious, too. Emily and Matt ate every bit.

"Now that's the spirit!" said Mrs. Brown. "Enjoy yourself today, I always say. Who knows what tomorrow will bring?"

Matt gulped. Mrs. Brown didn't realize how true her words were going to be. Everything would change on the *Titanic* in just a few hours. No one's life would ever be the same.

9

9:00 P.M.

"Where's the A La Carte restaurant?" Matt asked Mrs. Brown as soon as dinner was over. "We thought it would be fun to peek into it."

"Good idea. Have a look before bedtime. You're probably tired. I am for sure." Mrs. Brown yawned and stood up. They bid everyone at the table good night.

They returned to Mrs. Brown's stateroom, and she drew them a map. She put an X on the spot where they'd find the A La Carte restaurant.

"Good night, Mrs. Brown," said Matt, picking up the sled.

"Thank you for dinner and for telling Arthur to leave us alone, and for everything," said Emily. She hugged Mrs. Brown.

Mrs. Brown hugged Emily back. She shook hands with Matt. "Now, remember. Come see me tomorrow and we'll have dinner with the captain."

Mrs. Brown shut the door to her stateroom. Emily and Matt raced to the A La Carte restaurant. There was no one there except a few waiters cleaning up.

"Dinner is over," barked a waiter.

"We're looking for the captain," said Matt.

"He left. Hours ago."

"Oh no!" said Emily.

They darted out of the restaurant and back down the deck.

"Now what?" asked Matt.

"Now nothing. It's hopeless," said Emily. "The ship is huge. The captain could be anywhere. We'll never find him. And it's getting cold outside."

"It's getting late, too," groaned Matt.

They turned a corner. A bearded man in a dark uniform with shiny buttons, and a fancy cap was walking toward them. He looked like...

"The captain," whispered Emily.

The friends hurried over to him.

"Are you Captain Smith?" asked Matt.

The man nodded. "Yes. What can I do for you?"

"We have to ask you something. It's a matter of life and death. And you have to believe us. Please," said Emily.

"Go ahead," said the captain. "I'm listening."

"Could you slow the ship down? It's going to hit an iceberg very, very soon. Please be on the lookout."

The captain smiled. Then he patted Emily on the arm. "Now, my dear child. Nothing will happen. Even if the reports of icebergs in the area are true, we'll have enough time to steer the ship out of the way. And if we were to hit an iceberg, this ship is rock solid. Nothing will sink it. Now, off you go. You should both be in bed by now." The captain began to walk away.

Matt ran after him. "Wait, sir, please. If you don't slow the ship down, the *Titanic* will collide with an iceberg at 11:40 p.m. and sink less than three hours later. If you don't do something about it, I know you'll feel terrible when that happens."

The captain sighed. "I know you mean well. And I know you believe what you're telling me. I have a daughter and she has a vivid imagination like you. You should be enjoying the trip, not worrying about icebergs. It's not every day that a boy and girl travel on such a wonderful ship. I assure you, you will remember this voyage forever."

Emily gulped. "We'll remember the *Titanic*."

"The whole world will remember what happens tonight," said Matt.

The captain smiled, tipped his cap, and walked off.

10

9:30 P.M.

Emily sank into a deck chair. "I give up!" she said, throwing her hands up. "No one believes us. This ship is going under and we can't do anything to stop it."

"We can stop it! We have to stop it! I believe you!" called a girl. Emily and Matt looked up. It was Sally! She was racing down the deck in her nightgown.

"When I told my aunt about your little talking machine, she said I must have imagined it playing my voice back," said Sally. "She said no child could figure out how to do a trick like that, and that machine could never work. And then I knew. You are from the future. The *Titanic* is going to sink. When my aunt went to sleep, I tiptoed out of the cabin. I thought I'd never find you in time, but I have!"

"It's too late. No one believes us. The captain won't slow the ship down," said Matt.

"There's one more person to try. Let's talk to the wireless operator. Let's tell him to send a message and get help," said Sally. "I know where the wireless office is. Follow me."

The three friends dashed over to the office.

The wireless officer had piles of messages on his desk. He was transmitting them one by one.

"Please stop what you're doing," said Matt, huffing and out of breath. "Send an SOS. We're going to hit an iceberg in less than two hours!"

"Lots of people are going to drown unless you do something now," said Emily.

"It's all up to you," said Sally.

The wireless officer looked up from his stacks of messages. His face was red and angry.

"Get out of here!" he shouted. "Can't you see I'm busy? I have all these messages to send. If they don't go out, I'll be in big trouble. I have no time to play silly children's games."

"We're not silly," said Sally.

"And we're not kidding," said Emily.

"We're going to hit the iceberg at 11:40," said Matt. "There's no time left."

"If you three don't get out of here right now, I am going to pick you up one by one and toss you out," said the wireless officer, waving a fist at them.

Matt sighed. "Okay. We're going, but at 11:40 you'll see that this is no joke. The ship is doomed unless you do something fast."

But the wireless officer's only response was to shout "Get out! Get out! Get out!"

The three friends darted out of the office.

"I have to tell my aunt to wake up and get dressed," said Sally. "I'd better dress in something warm, too. We have to find a lifeboat. I don't want to drown. Are you going back to the future before the ship hits the iceberg?"

Matt and Emily glanced at the sled. There were no words in front telling them to leave.

"We don't know when we're leaving," said Matt. "We'll come with you now."

They all raced to Sally's cabin.

"Aunt Ellen, you must get up now. You have to get dressed. It's an emergency," cried Sally.

Sally's aunt rubbed her eyes and sat up in bed. "What's happened?" she asked.

"Nothing's happened yet, but soon the ship will hit an iceberg and start to sink," said Matt.

"Who are these children, Sally? Why are you running around with them? You're in your nightgown! Your mother would be appalled. It's late. Get back to bed this instant."

"I'm not getting into bed," said Sally. "I'm getting dressed and so should you. Matt, could you step outside while I get into my clothes?"

"Sure," said Matt.

"I'll wait outside with Matt," said Emily.

They waited outside Sally's cabin.

Matt and Emily heard Sally arguing with her aunt. Their voices were so loud that they could hear every word.

But no matter what Sally said, her aunt was not convinced that anything terrible was going to happen.

"They've been arguing for an hour," Emily whispered to Matt.

"I know. It must be close to 11:00 p.m. There's no time left!"

"Sally is beginning to sound desperate. How is she ever going to convince her aunt to leave her cabin?"

Sally sounded like she was about to cry. "Please, Aunt Ellen. I'll never ask you for anything else ever again, if you'll just do this one thing for me. Please. This is important. It's a matter of life and death."

"Sally, you are impossible," said her aunt.

"If I go upstairs with you for a few minutes, do you promise to be good for the rest of the voyage?"

"I'll be good as gold and you'll be glad we went."

"I doubt that. But I'll go up to the deck for a few minutes with you and your friends so I can get some rest."

11

11:30 PM

Sally opened the door. She was dressed in layers of clothes. "My aunt will be right out," said Sally.

"She has to hurry," said Matt. "The ship will hit the iceberg in ten minutes."

"She promised to be out right away," said Sally.

While they waited, another cabin door opened. Hilda Slayter stepped out of the cabin wearing a coat over her nightgown. She yawned as she looked up and down the hall.

"Miss Slayter, remember us? Emily and Matt?" called Emily.

"What's all the noise?" asked Hilda.

"The ship is headed straight for an iceberg. It's too late to stop it," said Matt.

"Are you sure?" said Hilda.

"We're positive," said Emily.

"I don't know what to do," said Hilda. "Florence is still asleep."

"Wake her up and get into a lifeboat," said Emily.

"But my dress. My jewels. How can I leave everything?"

"How can you take anything?" cried Emily. "Forget about the dress. Save yourself. Please!"

Hilda shook her head like she was trying to snap herself out of a bad dream. "You're right, of course. Thank you. Take care of yourselves."

Hilda dashed back into her cabin.

The friends could hear her call, "Florence, wake up. There's an emergency!"

Sally's aunt popped out of their cabin.

"Let's head for the boat deck," said Matt. "The lifeboats are there."

Everyone followed Matt up the stairs and to the forward part of the boat deck.

As they reached the deck, they felt a jolt. Then there was silence.

"Why is it so quiet all of a sudden?" asked Sally.

"I think the engines have stopped," said Matt.

"Oh, my goodness!" said Sally. "We've hit the iceberg."

"I hardly felt anything," said Sally's aunt. "You must be mistaken. I'll ask this steward what he knows."

Sally's aunt approached a young steward. "The children think we've hit an iceberg. We haven't, have we?"

The steward gulped. "Something did happen. I'm not sure what, ma'am. Maybe you'd better stay on deck till we can find out more."

"Oh my," said Sally's aunt. "Something terrible *has* happened. I don't know how you children knew, but—"

People began to run up on to the deck.

There were parents and children, old people and young people. Some were dressed.

Some were still in their nightclothes with a coat slung over them. Everyone clustered around the deck.

"Did you hear it?" said an older woman. "Did you feel it?"

"It can't be!" said her husband.

"Not the *Titanic*!" said a tall woman wrapped in furs. "It's not possible."

"It *is* possible," said a familiar voice. It was Mrs. Brown. She hurried over to where Emily, Matt, Sally, and her aunt were huddled. "You two knew something was going to happen tonight. I don't know how, but you were right. We must speak to someone from the crew."

Everyone peered around but they couldn't see anyone from the crew. Emily and Matt looked at each other. The *Titanic* was going to sink fast. People had to get into the lifeboats soon.

Just then an officer dashed up to the deck. "Ladies and gentlemen," he announced. "I'm going to have to ask you to head toward the lifeboats. Women and children first. There is no cause for panic, but please move quickly."

"Hurry," said Mrs. Brown. "There's a lifeboat here. Let's all get in."

But before they could move, Emily poked Matt in the side. "Look at the sled!"

Shimmery gold words were forming on the front of the sled.

You tried your best.
You let them know.
But now it's time
For you to go.

"We have to go home," said Matt.

"Goodbye, Sally. Goodbye, Mrs. Brown. Goodbye, everyone! Good luck!" said Emily as she hopped on the sled behind Matt.

The sled rose in the air. Everyone was so busy scrambling into lifeboats that few people looked up to see it flying. The only ones who did were Sally and Mrs. Brown.

As the sled rose above the *Titanic*, Sally called out, "Remember me!"

Mrs. Brown said, "Well, I'll be..." Then she stepped into lifeboat Number Six.

Soon the sled was high over the *Titanic*. Below, the huge ship was leaning into the sea. It was starting to sink.

Emily closed her eyes. "It's so sad. There was nothing we could do to save the ship."

"But maybe we helped Sally, her aunt, Mrs. Brown, and Hilda. Maybe even that boy Lou remembered our warning and jumped into a lifeboat."

"I hope so," said Emily as the sled burst into the fluffy white cloud.

Before they knew it, they were back in Emily's tower room. The two friends slid off the sled.

"I can't believe it," said Emily. "We were there when the iceberg hit the *Titanic*!"

"I wish we could have done something to make the captain stop the ship."

"I know," said Emily. "I wonder if our friends made it back safely."

"Me, too."

"Let's look up the names of the survivors on the Internet," said Emily.

Emily and Matt raced downstairs and turned on Emily's computer. They Googled the words "*Titanic* survivors."

"I'm almost too nervous to look," said Emily. "I liked some of those people we met on the *Titanic*. I hope they didn't drown."

Matt stared at the screen. "I don't see a

boy named Lou listed in Third Class. There's no record of him at all. Maybe Lou was his nickname."

"We'll never know," said Emily sadly. "Look, Matt. It says here that Captain Smith went down with the ship, and Mr. and Mrs. Straus decided to stay on the ship and let younger people take their place on the lifeboats. They were so kind." She sniffed back a tear. "I'll think of them whenever I go to Macy's in New York. I wish they had known that their store would still be around today."

"Look!" said Matt, pointing at the list.

"Yahoo!" cried Emily. "There's Hilda Slayter's name!"

"And Mrs. Brown," said Matt. "And there's a Sally from Second Class and an Ellen from Second Class, too. It looks like most of the first-class kids survived!"

Emily smiled. Then she grabbed her sketchbook and drew a picture of the *Titanic*. Beside it she wrote the names of all the people they'd met.

"I'll never forget each person we got to know on the *Titanic*," she said.

Matt nodded. "And whenever I look at my model of the *Titanic*, I'll remember what happened to us while we were there. That was an awesome adventure, and that was an awesome ship!"

MORE ABOUT...

After their adventure, Matt and Emily wanted to know more about the *Titanic*. Turn the page for their favourite facts.

Matt's Top Ten Facts

1. The word titanic means huge, gigantic, or colossal. The *Titanic* was all that! It was as high as an eleven—storey apartment building.

2. Five people on the *Titanic* were born in Canada, 35 lived in Canada, and 81 were on their way there.

3. There were as many as a dozen dogs on the *Titanic*. The crew took them for walks every day. Only two dogs survived.

4. Before the *Titanic* left Southampton, England on its way to New York, it almost collided with a ship called the *New York*.

5. Captain Smith took a more southerly route than usual because he had received warnings of icebergs. But he never slowed the ship down.

And our *Titanic* adventure was huge, gigantic, and colossal.
—E.

6. When the iceberg hit, John Phillips, the First Wireless Officer, sent an SOS message by Morse code. SOS was a new signal invented to alert the receiver of the need for immediate help.

7. Guglielmo Marconi, the inventor of the wireless telegraph, was supposed to sail from New York to England on the *Titanic* 's return trip.

8. The *Titanic* had sixteen lifeboats and four collapsible boats, only enough for half of the 2,200 passengers.

9. In 1985 Dr. Robert Ballard discovered the remains of the *Titanic* deep in the Atlantic. He proved that the ship had broken in two before sinking.

10. The last survivor of the *Titanic*, Millvina Dean, died in May 2009. She was just nine weeks old when she and her family boarded the ship as third-class passengers.

Millvina lived to be almost 100!

—E.

Emily's Top Ten Facts

1. Some of the cargo the *Titanic* carried was: five grand pianos, twelve cases of ostrich plumes, three cases of shelled walnuts, twenty-five cans of sardines, and fifteen cases of rabbit hair.

2. Neither of the lookouts on the *Titanic* (Frederick Fleet or Reginald Lee) had binoculars. They'd misplaced them in the rush to get on board.

If they hadn't, who knows if things would have turned out differently?
—M.

3. The *Titanic* was one of the few ships in those days that let kids eat with their parents in the dining room. French ships didn't even allow infants on board.

4. Some of the world's richest people travelled on the *Titanic*, like Colonel and Mrs. Astor and Benjamin Guggenheim. Of those three, Mrs. Astor was the only one to survive.

5. Captain Smith ordered the crew to send white rockets into the air. He hoped that some ship would notice and see that the *Titanic* was sinking, but no ship noticed.

6. The first Macy's parade took place in November 1924, twelve years after the *Titanic* sunk.

7. Violet Jessup, a stewardess on the *Titanic*, survived. Four years later, during World War I, she sailed on the *Britannic*. It sank too, but Violet came through again!

   Lucky Violet!
   —M.

8. One of the wireless operators, Harold Bride, survived the disaster. The other, Jack Phillips, did not.

9. Some men, like Jack Thayer and Harold Bride, clung to an overturned lifeboat for hours. It's amazing that they managed to hold on until the *Carpathia* arrived to rescue the survivors.

10. The *Carpathia* arrived in New York on April 18, 1912, at 9:00 p.m., with 705 *Titanic* survivors.

So You Want to Know...

FROM AUTHOR FRIEDA WISHINSKY

When I was writing this book, my friends wanted to know more about the *Titanic* and icebergs, as well as what happened to the survivors in my story.

I told them that some of the characters in *SOS! Titanic!* were made-up but that others—like Mrs. Brown, Ida and Isidor Straus, Captain Smith, and Hilda Slayter—were real people. Mrs. Brown and Hilda Slayter survived the disaster. The others did not.

Here are some other questions I answered:

Where did the *Titanic* sink?

The *Titanic* sank approximately 640 km (400 miles) off the coast of Newfoundland.

Why are there so many icebergs in that part of the Atlantic in April?

The iceberg the *Titanic* struck was probably part of a glacier from Greenland that had broken off at sea. Icebergs like these are common along the coast of Newfoundland from March to July. Winds and currents determine how many icebergs will drift down, and conditions change every year.

Why didn't the people on the *Titanic* see the iceberg earlier?

This iceberg may have been a "blue berg." An iceberg is called that when it rolls over because of strong currents. Then the newly exposed part is darker than the rest of the iceberg. That would make the iceberg difficult to see, especially since most of the iceberg is under water.

What does SOS stand for?

Many people think SOS stands for Save Our Ship, but it's simply an easy signal in Morse Code—three dots, three dashes, and three dots—repeated over and over without a pause in between.

What happened after the *Titanic* survivors arrived in New York?

There was an investigation into the accident, and the White Star Line chartered a steamer in Halifax to search the scene of the disaster. The steamer found 306 bodies, most floating in life preservers. They buried some people at sea and brought others back to Halifax. In the end, 150 people were buried in Halifax while the rest were buried elsewhere.

What was Hilda Slayter's life like before and after the *Titanic*?

Hilda was born in Halifax, the tenth child in a well-to-do family. Hilda travelled extensively with her family in Europe as a child. She studied music and hoped to have a career as a concert singer, but it didn't work out. Instead, she decided to marry Harry Lacon, the son of a British politician, who lived in British Columbia.

When the *Titanic* struck the iceberg, Hilda bundled up in layers of clothing. She shared her clothing with other passengers in her lifeboat. Her beautiful wedding dress was lost at sea.

After reaching New York, she travelled to British Columbia and married Harry. They had one son. During World War One, while Harry was fighting overseas, Hilda and her son returned to Halifax. They were there during the terrible Halifax explosion. For the second time, Hilda lived through a major disaster.

What was Mrs. Brown really like?

She was a strong advocate for women's rights, literacy, education, and human rights. She even ran for the Senate in the United States, eight years before women won the right to vote.

When the *Titanic* hit the iceberg, Mrs. Brown helped people into lifeboats. Eventually she boarded lifeboat Number Six. She helped row the lifeboat and kept everyone's spirits up during that awful night. On the *Carpathia*, she assisted and comforted people, too. She later helped form a Survivor's Committee, and raised money for poor survivors.

Mrs. Brown died in 1932. In 1960, a stage musical called *The Unsinkable Molly Brown* was produced. It was full of inaccurate information about her life, but it was very popular. A few years later, a film based on the musical was also released.

Coming next in the
Canadian Flyer Adventures Series...

Canadian Flyer Adventures
#15

Make It
Fair!

Emily and Matt help Nellie McClung win
women's right to vote in Manitoba.

For a sneak peek at the latest book in the series, visit:
www.owlkids.com
and click on the red maple leaf!

The *Canadian Flyer* *Adventures* Series

#1 Beware, Pirates!

#2 Danger, Dinosaurs!

#3 Crazy for Gold

#4 Yikes, Vikings!

#5 Flying High!

#6 Pioneer Kids

#7 Hurry, Freedom

#8 A Whale Tale

#9 All Aboard!

#10 Lost in the Snow

#11 Far from Home

#12 On the Case

#13 Stop that Stagecoach!

#14 SOS! Titanic!

Upcoming Book

Look out for the next book that will take Emily and Matt on a new adventure:

#15 Make It Fair!

And more to come!

More Praise for the Series

"[Emily and Matt] learn more than they ever could have from a history textbook. Every book in this new series promises to shed light on a different chapter of Canadian history."
~ *MONTREAL GAZETTE*

"Readers are in for a great adventure."
~ *EDMONTON'S CHILD*

"This series makes Canadian history fun, exciting and accessible."
~ *CHRONICLE HERALD (HALIFAX)*

"[An] enthralling series for junior-school readers."
~ *HAMILTON SPECTATOR*

"...highly entertaining, very educational but not too challenging. A terrific new series."
~ *RESOURCE LINKS*

"This wonderful new Canadian historical adventure series combines magic and history to whisk young readers away on adventure...A fun way to learn about Canada's past."
~ *BC PARENT*

"Highly recommended."
~ *CM: CANADIAN REVIEW OF MATERIALS*

Teacher Resource Guides now available
online. Please visit our website at
www.owlkids.com
and click on the red maple leaf to
download tips and ideas for using the
series in the classroom.

About the Author

Frieda Wishinsky, a former teacher, is an award-winning picture- and chapter-book author, who has written many beloved and bestselling books for children. Frieda enjoys using humor and history in her work, while exploring new ways to tell a story. Her books have earned much critical praise, including a nomination for the Governor General's Award. She is the author of *Please, Louise; You're Mean, Lily Jean; Each One Special;* and *What's the Matter with Albert?* among others. Originally from New York, Frieda now lives in Toronto.

About the Illustrator

Jean-Paul Eid has been drawing for as long as he can remember. From a very young age he dreamed of becoming a comic book artist, and liked to doodle cartoon characters of his teachers in the margins of his school workbooks. At the age of 20, he published his first comic in a magazine. Since then, he has published four award-winning graphic novels as well as several books for children. He has also done illustrations for museums, children's magazines, and film productions. Jean-Paul lives in Montreal, Quebec, with his two children, Mathilde and Axel.